MR.WRONG

by Roger Hargreaves

WORLD INTERNATIONAL PUBLISHING LIMITED
MANCHESTER

Whatever Mr Wrong did was absolutely, totally, completely, utterly wrong.

However hard he tried, he just couldn't do anything right.

Just look at his house!

One fine morning Mr Wrong woke up.

He hadn't slept very well because of the way he'd made his bed the day before.

He jumped out of bed, fell over (twice), put on his shoes (on the wrong feet), went to the bathroom (tripping over the bathmat), squeezed out some toothpaste (on to the wrong side of his toothbrush), cleaned his teeth (ouch) and went downstairs.

Bump, bump, bump, bump, bump, bump, bump!

Not a very good start to the day.

In fact, his usual wrong start to the day.

In his kitchen, Mr Wrong poured some milk on to his cornflakes.

And missed!

As he sat in his kitchen, that fine morning, eating his dry cornflakes, he sighed.

"Oh dear," he thought, "I do so wish that everything I do wasn't quite so absolutely, totally, completely, utterly wrong."

So, after breakfast, he went for a walk in order to think how he could solve his problem.

It took him ten minutes to get out of the house, because he kept trying to open his front door outwards instead of inwards!

As he walked along he passed a worm.

"Good morning, Dog," he said.

The worm grinned.

He was used to Mr Wrong.

He met a postman.

"Good morning, Mr Wrong," called the postman cheerfully.

"Good morning, Doctor," replied Mr Wrong.

Oh dear!

He met old Mrs Twinkle who lived down the lane.

"Good morning, Mr Wrong," she smiled.

"Good morning, Mr Twinkle," replied Mr Wrong.

Oh dear!

And then he met somebody he'd never met before.

Somebody who sort of looked like him, but didn't.

"Good morning, Sir," said that somebody.

"Good morning, Madam," replied Mr Wrong. "I'm Mr Wrong."

"I guessed that," replied the person. "Well, I'm Mr Right."

"Now tell me," he went on, "why are you walking along looking so miserable?"

"Because," replied Mr Wrong, "I can't do anything right!"

"In which case," said Mr Right, "we'd better do something about it. Follow me."

And off he set.

And off set Mr Wrong.

In the opposite direction!

Mr Right hurried back, and turned him round.

"This way," he said, and they walked together to where Mr Right lived.

It was a house which somehow looked something like Mr Wrong's house.

But different.

Mr Right took Mr Wrong into his living room.

"I think," he said, "that the only way you are ever going to change is for you to come and live with me for a while, and you may end up being not quite so absolutely, totally, completely, utterly wrong about everything."

"Sit down," he said, "and we'll talk about it."

Mr Wrong sat down.

And missed!

Mr Wrong stayed with Mr Right for a month.

And, during that time, he changed.

After one week he was slightly less wrong than he had been before.

After two weeks he was even more slightly less wrong than he had been before.

And, after a whole four weeks, he was a changed Mr Man.

You could hardly tell the difference between him and Mr Right.

Don't you agree?

Mr Right was delighted.

"Told you," he cried. "Told you that everything about you might end up being not quite so absolutely, totally, completely, utterly wrong!"

"In fact," he continued, "you've really turned out all right!"

Mr Wrong blushed.

It was quite the nicest thing anyone had ever said to him in the whole of his life.

And he went home.

And lived happily, and right, ever after.

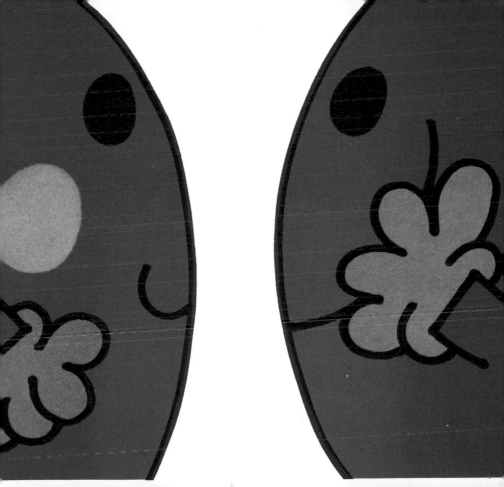

Now.

You probably think that's the end of the story.

Don't you?

Well it isn't!

And the reason it isn't is because of what happened to Mr Right.

The trouble was, you see, that the longer Mr Wrong had stayed with Mr Right, and the more right Mr Wrong became, the more wrong Mr Right had become.

Isn't that extraordinary?

"Oh dear," Mr Right sighed. "My plan didn't quite work out the way I'd planned it after all."

And he went to bed.

In the bath!